MURDER HAMMERS!

NIKI DUPRE SHORT STORIES BOOK 16

JIM RILEY

To the Most Beautiful

You Always Were

You Always Will Be

MYSTERIES BY JIM RILEY

Hawk Theriot & Kristi Blocker full-length Mysteries

Murder in the Atchafalaya

Murder in Lake Palourde

Murder by Rougarou

Hawk Theriot & Kristi Blocker Short Story Mysteries

Murder at the Haunted House

Murder in the Cemetery

Wade Dalton & Sam Cates full-length Mysteries

The Girl in the Woods

Murder by Moccasin

Stranded in the Swamp

Wade Dalton & Sam Cates Short Story Mysteries

The Philandering Father

Murder for Lease

Murder and Rubber Chicken

Murder of the Mayor

Niki Dupre full-length Mysteries

Murder on Spirit Island

Murder at Tiger Eye

Murder & Billy Bailey

Murder in Louisiana Politics

Murder Under the Sun

Murder Goes to the Dogs

Murder for Peace

Murder &Needles

Niki Dupre Short Story Mysteries

Murder in the Cards

Murder of the Sheriff

Murder on Autopilot

Murder for Art

Murder Explodes with a Bang

Murder on Loan

Murder at the Washateria

Murder by Mistake

Murder Weighs on You

Murder Burns

Murder by Decapitation

Murder in the Hills

Murder Steals

Murder & 'Yer Out!'

Murder Minus Toes

Murder Hammers!

Murder Wears Blue

CHAPTER ONE

Keith and Murray Clement were not the most brilliant thieves in Livingston Parish. They hadn't done well in school. Keith, one year older than his brother, set the example for Murray. His leadership led both to drop out of Denham Springs High School before graduation. He also provided the path to the use of methamphetamines and marijuana.

Though they had no steady employment, the brothers paid for their vices through petty thefts. Nothing big. Tools were easy to peddle on Craigslist. And most couldn't be traced back to the original owners.

Even with their combined acumen in the lowest percentile in South Louisiana, the brothers recognized a golden opportunity. Hurricane Brenda ravished the southern bayous and marshes of the Pelican State with Category three winds as far north as the Mississippi border. Baton Rouge and the surrounding parishes bore the brunt of the wide bands of destruction. A mandatory evacuation left the city of Watson deserted.

Never known to obey any orders, Keith and Murray hunkered down in their dilapidated shack along Bayou Delaune. The rickety structure had no electricity before the storm, so the power outage had little effect. How the hut survived the gale force winds was a miracle.

The brothers discovered they were left alone in the small suburb north of Denham Springs. All the homeowners had left before the storm and were banned from returning for three days after it blew through.

That meant thousands of tools were left behind with nobody watching. A gold mine awaited, and Keith and Murray took advantage.

With no electricity to power the alarm systems, the brother struck house after house. They took every tool in the flooded garages and sheds. Saws, wrenches, hammers, socket sets, screwdrivers, drills. Anything that could quickly be sold at bargain-basement prices on the worldwide web.

Some homes had standing water. Not clear tap water, but that filled with debris, mud, and God only knows what else. That didn't deter the brothers. They waded through the muck and mire to reap the treasures the owners had so graciously left behind in their hasty departure.

The old Ford F150 wasn't pretty. The rust and Bond-O patches marred its beauty. However, it sat twenty-six inches higher than the factory standard and motored through the high patches of water with ease.

The only drawback was the small bed in the back of the pickup. The brothers were forced to make many trips back to the shack to unload their loot.

On the seventh trip of the second day, the unthinkable happened.

CHAPTER TWO

At the subdivision entrance, a parish squad car awaited the old pickup truck and the Clement brothers. Keith, as usual, sat at the steering wheel.

He thought about turning around. Then, he remembered the only other exit had more than eight feet of water from Bayou Delaune blocking it. There were no alternatives.

Keith may have been deficient in many areas of life, but his will to survive topped his fellow men. There was no way he would let a parish Deputy interfere with the chance of a lifetime to strike it rich. He looked at his brother, who could not take his eyes off the flashing lights of the police car.

"Hold on," Keith muttered before gunning the engine.

The F-150, with its souped-up engine, ripped through the last hundred yards to the exit. Straight at the squad car parked sideways.

The wide-eyed deputy, George Allen, saw the powerful vehicle racing toward him. He couldn't believe his eyes. At the last second, George slammed the car in drive and jerked forward. He almost made it.

The pickup hit his car a foot behind the rear wheel. The police automobile spun around one hundred and eighty degrees, facing the opposite direction when it came to rest.

Keith lost control of the pickup truck. The impact forced his body into the steering wheel. Murray's forehead slammed into the windshield. Neither brother had prepared for the truck dropping from the road to the deep ditch on the other side.

With the engine submerged, the old truck went nowhere. The airbags deployed, temporarily trapping both brothers. Not that it mattered. Murray bent over unconscious in the passenger seat, blood pouring from the cut high on his head.

Keith felt the two broken ribs sending jarring pain throughout his torso. He turned his head to see George Allen approaching, a scowl on his face, and a 9mm Glock in his hand.

CHAPTER THREE

AFTER THE TOW truck pulled the pickup from the ditch, Detective Bruce Daniels discovered the stolen tools in its bed. He didn't need to utilize his twelve years of experience to make a connection of the large number of items to the vacant houses in the subdivision.

He couldn't pull all the stolen loot out of the truck at that moment. Instead, the detective took several photographs of the merchandise, and told the tow truck to take the pickup to the police garage in Watson. He then walked over to the ambulance holding Murray in the rear compartment.

"Has anyone read the Miranda rights to you?"

Murray looked at him with unseeing eyes.

Bruce realized the droopy-eyed thief hadn't comprehended the question. The younger brother couldn't communicate.

Bruce walked over to the older brother. While still in considerable pain, Keith maintained his limited cognitive skills. The detective confirmed the elder brother had heard and understood his civil rights.

"Where did you get those tools?" Bruce asked.

"We bought them off the Internet," Keith replied.

"Why are they in the back of your truck?"

"Ain't got around to unloading them yet. That's where we were going when the cop car ran into us."

Bruce laughed. "Yeah, it's a shame he hit the front grill of your truck with the trunk of his car. I didn't know George was that talented."

"We tried to dodge him. That's why it looks the way it looks," Keith moaned.

The detective couldn't contain his grin.

"That dog won't hunt. Let's get back to the tools. Which houses did you take them from?"

"We ain't took no tools from no houses."

"Do you remember when you walked through them?" Bruce asked.

Keith's look told it all. He knew that some homes had only mud, no water. His and his brother's bootprints were all over the garages.

"I see you're not wearing gloves. I'd bet your fingerprints are scattered throughout this whole subdivision," Bruce said.

Keith could only hang his head. He knew he and his brother had been caught. However, he couldn't see the surprise that lay ahead.

CHAPTER FOUR

The forensic technician, Melanie Keys, thought the assigned job beneath her stature. Almost insulting. She had been instructed to inspect hundreds of tools recovered from the Clement's truck and shack. The highly skilled technician tried to match each tool to a homeowner in the Richmond Place Subdivision.

Some were easy. The power tools, drills, circular saws, and chainsaws had serial numbers. Many owners hadn't sold, swapped, or lost them until the adventures of Keith and Murray.

Others were impossible to trace. Hammers, screwdrivers, sockets, and wrenches bore no unique numbers. Melanie knew there was no scientific way to place those tools with their respective owners unless there was photographic evidence. She was at a loss of how to sort through over a hundred hammers that all looked similar. None had distinguishing marks. Except one. The marks on it stood out in a spectacular fashion. It was covered with human blood.

CHAPTER FIVE

BECAUSE HE HAD BEEN the first and only detective at the scene for the arrest of the Clement brothers, Bruce Daniels drew the task. He needed to find the source of the blood.

The lean detective started with the first house in the neighborhood. Though the waters of Bayou Delaune had receded, the mud and muck remained, making every step a chore.

The first house on the block revealed no signs of foul play. Nor the second. Nor the third. Nor the sixteenth.

Bruce moved forward to the second block. He found no results to help identify the source of the blood. The humidity blanketed him like a wet sheet. Sweat poured down his face onto his clothes. Not that it mattered. His shirt and trousers were already soaked from perspiration. The sweat from his face only added to the clinging nature of the fabrics. Bruce took a break after the second block. He debated the usefulness of continuing the search. Though Melanie Cotton had sworn the blood was recent, the detective didn't trust her logic. After all, dried blood was dried blood. How could Melanie determine if it was fresh or old? He knew the youngster was good at her job, but this is one time he doubted the veracity of her findings. Especially, if it meant trudging through mud for the rest of this blistering hot day.

After a cold Dr Pepper, Bruce resumed the investigation. On the fourth block, he smelled the object of his search. Though the mud and debris left from the storm reeked, nothing smelled the same as the odor of decaying flesh. Having the painful experience of being in the vicinity of rotting bodies before, the detective immediately recognized the source of the putrid emanations.

He found the body of Bobby Burns by the back door, the back of his head caved in.

CHAPTER SIX

"Niki, I need your help."

The most famous private investigator in Louisiana, Niki Dupre, knew the voice on the other end of the cell phone connection. She had heard it so often in the thirteen-year-old girl's class at Zoar Baptist Church in Central.

"Miss Pattie Grace, what can I do to help?"

"It's Bobby. They think I killed him."

"Whoa! Wait a minute! Mr. Bobby is dead?" The astonished investigator asked.

"They found him at the house after the storm. They said my fingerprints are on the hammer that killed him."

Niki took a few seconds to absorb the words. Bobby and Pattie Grace Burns were the most respected couple at the church where she grew up. Bobby was a retired Navy Admiral, and Niki had never heard anyone say a bad word about him.

As respected as he had been, Pattie Grace was even more so. She was the ideal role model for the young girls transitioning to teenagers. Niki and her classmates had confided their deepest secrets to the saintly lady.

"When did they find Bobby?" Niki asked.

"This morning. A detective found him in our house. Somebody hit him with a hammer."

"Why was he there? There's still a mandatory evacuation order in effect for Watson."

"You know Bobby. He can... Could be so stubborn. He never listened to me no matter how much I made sense."

"Are you saying he refused to leave with the storm coming?"

"I begged him to come with me to Bernice. We both have relatives here. He kept arguing with me and wouldn't leave. Now, he's dead."

"How did your prints get on the hammer?" Niki asked.

"Bobby nailed up plywood over our windows with it. He left it on the kitchen counter when he got through. You know Bobby. He never put his tools away when he got finished with them."

"So, you picked it up to put it back in the toolbox?"

"No. I picked it up and threatened to throw it at him if he didn't leave town with me."

"Did you throw it?" Niki asked hesitantly.

"I wanted to, but I love that stubborn fool, even if he wanted to hunker down and ride out the hurricane."

"Miss Pattie Grace, I have to be certain. Did you hit Mr. Bobby in anger?"

"God knows, I was mad enough. But I didn't. I left right before the storm hit Watson. It was already on land north of Grande Isle. I barely got out in time."

"Are you under arrest?"

"Not yet. I'm still in Bernice with Linda, my cousin. The detective said he might come up here to get me, though."

"Stay there until you hear from me. I can access the files and see if the detective has anything other than your prints for evidence."

"What if they come to arrest me?"

"I'll talk to the detective on the case. If it comes to that, we'll make arrangements for you to return. Until then, stay put."

"Niki, I didn't kill Bobby. There were lots of times I was tempted, but I didn't do it."

CHAPTER SEVEN

"What have you found so far?" Niki asked her partner, Donna Cross.

The hourglass blonde, a few years younger than Niki, could hack into any database in the world without leaving perceptible tracks. She had infiltrated the Sheriff's system so many times, Donna created her private username and password. Niki asked her to find out what she could about the murder of Bobby Burns.

"Bruce Daniels is the detective in charge," Donna replied. "He's the one who called Mrs. Burns."

"Everybody calls her Miss Pattie Grace. I didn't know her last name until after I was out of her class."

"I was never much into Sunday School. They kept talking about all the dead people in the Bible. I'd rather talk about folks who are still alive."

"Don't you believe Jesus is alive?"

"Sure," Donna answered. "But you know what I mean. Who cares how old Methuselah was or if the fish that swallowed Jonah was really a whale?"

"You might have missed the point of those stories.

If you had Miss Pattie Grace as the teacher, you would've liked going a lot more."

"Anyway, according to the report Daniels filed, the hammer is definitely the murder weapon. He found three sets of prints; Bobby Burns's, Pattie Grace's, and Keith Clement's. Keith is the guy who had the hammer in the back of his truck, along with his brother, Murray."

"If they found it in Keith's possession, why isn't he the prime suspect?"

"He's right up there with Pattie Grace. But they found hundreds of tools in his truck and his home. Daniels thinks Keith and his brother are small-time thieves who exploited the aftermath of the hurricane to steal tools from vacated houses."

"If they encountered Mr. Bobby unexpectedly at his house, it might have turned into a fracas and gotten out of hand. Keith might have killed Mr. Bobby."

"It says here that Keith is only five-eight and weighs a hundred and forty-five pounds. His brother is smaller."

"Mr. Bobby was over six feet tall and weighed over two hundred pounds. Unless he changed since I saw him last, not an ounce of it was fat."

"It would've been difficult for those little guys to take him out, I would think."

"Plus, Mr. Bobby was military his whole life. He knew how to defend himself."

"Anything else you want to know from the report?" Donna asked.

"Not right now, but maybe later. Any interesting findings from the autopsy?"

"Daniels hasn't gotten it yet, but I pulled a copy from the coroner's database."

"You're gonna get in trouble one of these days pilfering through those systems. They're going to catch you, eventually."

"Not a chance," Donna laughed. "Have you met the geniuses guarding those systems? A truant third-grader could bypass their security."

"Anyway, how long will it take you to get into the coroner's records?"

"Already there. What do you want to know?"

Niki's admiration for her friend's abilities rose to a new level, if that was possible.

"Anything of interest?" The strawberry blonde asked.

"Looks like Mr. Burns had something with peanuts, shrimp, and peppers about six to nine hours prior to death."

"Any other injuries in addition to the blow to his head?"

"Nope. That was it. One whack, and that's all it took."

CHAPTER EIGHT

"Bruce, this is Niki Dupre. Pattie Grace asked me to look into her husband's murder."

"Do you mean the one she committed?" The parish detective responded over Niki's cell phone.

"Have you already made up your mind?"

"Not one hundred percent. Maybe ninety-five or so. This looks like an easy case for a change."

"What about the Clement brothers? Didn't you find the murder weapon in their possession?"

"The way I figure it, the victim was killed before the storm. They said they weren't in the subdivision until the hurricane passed."

"What gives you that idea? Do you have the estimated time of death from the coroner?"

"Not yet," Daniels admitted. "It takes a while for those guys to get a report to us."

"So, why do you think Mr. Bobby died before the storm hit?"

"Common sense. That's something you amateurs could use a little bit of."

Niki ignored the slight aspersion to her profession. She had to become accustomed to public police officers thinking less than kindly of private investigators.

"If he died before the storm, why do you think Pattie Grace killed him?"

"Just a crazy thought," Daniels paused. "Or perhaps, it could be her fingerprints on the murder weapon. Or it could be that she admitted getting into an argument with her husband right before she fled to North Louisiana to remove suspicion."

"Do you think she's strong enough to bash his head in?"

"Who told you that. We haven't released the details of the murder to the public yet."

"It doesn't matter how I found out. Pattie Grace is a petite woman. I don't see how she could have done it."

"She did. One of her kids might have helped. I don't know. The only thing I know is that she's guilty."

"How FAST CAN you pull up info on Pattie Grace's kids?" Niki asked Donna after she disconnected with Bruce Daniels.

"Already got it," Donna beamed. "What do you want to know?"

"Give me all you have."

Donna provided sketches of the kids, though none were children.

Mary, the eldest of the Burns clan, was the most gregarious. She loved people. She loved interacting with them. The oldest daughter used her natural inclinations to manage more than a dozen payday loan businesses in South Louisiana. Freckled like her mother, Mary's smile was the first thing noticed by most. Unfortunately, chain-smoking created severe health problems for the businesswoman.

Gary came next to the Burns family. He followed his father into the Navy with many of the same traits as his sister, including an outgoing personality and freckles. His career was on the fast track until a crippling accident. While at sea, Gary worked below deck in the boiler rooms. During rough waters in the South

China Sea, a faulty valve failed, sending scalding steam over the sailor's body. With much encouragement from Admiral Bobby Burns, the Navy granted Gary a full pension and disability benefits. He had relocated from Watson to Bernice, close to his cousins.

Donald came next in line. He didn't have freckles and was more reserved than his older siblings. He also had an independent streak, which didn't bold well when he followed Bobby and Gary into military service. If not for actions taken by his father, the second son would have been ousted from the Navy on more than one occasion.

Dena was the baby of the family. Her faith was her life, and most of her perspectives were shaped through that prism. Fittingly, she worked at a Baptist Church on the outskirts of Watson as the Office Manager.

"So, which of them could have murdered their father?" Niki asked when Donna finished.

"Well," Donna said while glancing at her laptop before continuing. "We know it wasn't Gary unless he made a special trip to Watson. I can't answer for the others yet."

"Find out if any of them bought gas or left a trail close to their parents' house."

"Okay, what will you be doing?" Donna asked.

"I'm gonna take a look at the crime scene."

CHAPTER TEN

THE YELLOW TAPE remained around the perimeter of the house. Niki ducked under it and entered through the open garage, one of those broken into by the Clement brothers according to Bruce Daniels's report.

Water no longer covered the interior. Niki could make out the traffic marks made by the detective and the forensic technicians. Bobby's body had been found close to the back door.

The private investigator didn't hurry. She stopped and searched, though she was unsure exactly what she was seeking. In her experience, there were times she had not realized the significance of her findings until much later.

Niki walked to approximately where she thought the victim died, about two feet from the rear exit. Nothing seemed out of place, other than the knowledge a human being had lost his life at this spot. The investigator stood still for more than six minutes before seeing the first significant evidence.

Extending only three feet from the exterior wall, a partition separated the eating area from the door. On it, Niki found blood spray. It hadn't been mentioned in the official documents, causing the strawberry blonde a concern. She moved within a foot of the tiny beads to confirm her suspicions.

Those droplets told the investigator new information. The killer had quickly drawn the hammer back for a second blow, then found it unnecessary.

She remembered the brothers claimed they had found the hammer in the garage. Why had the killer taken it there? Did Pattie Grace know where Bobby kept the tool? Were the brothers lying?

Bobby had been struck on the back of his head. That meant he had been headed to the rear yard and Bayou Delaune.

Niki stepped through the still-open door. Immediately, the brutal destruction of Hurricane Brenda made her stop. Two mighty oak trees lay on their sides, uprooted by the Category three winds. The six-foot privacy fence no longer stood erect, the individual planks strewn throughout the yard. Leaves had been stripped from the limbs and piled in layers as the water receded.

Niki picked her way down to the large pier over the Bayou. The roof was now a memory. The T-shaped base stretched ten feet from the bank. The 'T' stood twelve feet wide.

Two thirty-gallon solar powered fish feeders sat on each end. The panel and dials were missing from the one to her left. The other appeared to have survived the storm intact. She walked to it, and after studying the control buttons for a few seconds, hit one. Small granules spewed from the circular drama over the water. The surface roiled with whiskers. The catfish had not been displaced by Hurricane Brenda. They had returned to a familiar feeding spot.

Niki lifted the lid of the feed container. Pellets filled it almost to the brim. She then checked the container that had been damaged by the hurricane. It was full all the way to the top.

When the investigator turned, she caught movement in a window in the house sitting on the high adjoining lot. It was brief, but certain. Since the evacuation order remained in effect, no one should have been there. Niki first thought a looter had broken into the home. But something about that scenario didn't ring true.

She walked back up the hill to Bobby's house. An upturned trashcan lay on its side by the back door. Niki instinctively reached down, and set it up right. On top were empty bags of catfish pellets. Niki paid them no mind. She focused on the movement at the house next door.

CHAPTER ELEVEN

THE HOUSE APPEARED to be vacant until Niki reached the front porch. She saw a light shining through the blinds covering the windows. With the power still off, she wondered how that was possible without a portable generator. She heard none.

The investigator rang the doorbell from rote instincts, although knowing it was a useless effort. The bell couldn't work without electricity.

To her surprise, she heard the chimes inside. Her curiosity grew. Despite the ringing, Niki received no reply.

Niki's thoughts of a looter returned. But there was no vehicle in the driveway. The investigator turned and looked up and down the street. She saw no automobiles save her own Ford Explorer.

Niki walked to the two-car garage. The door didn't budge. No one had jimmied it and parked inside.

She went back to the front door and again rang the bell. Still no answer. Niki rapped on the door hard enough that anyone inside had to hear it. No response.

Niki hadn't become the most successful private investigator in Louisiana by being timid. She stepped over the fallen fence on the side of the house and went to the back door.

She looked around before knocking. From this vantage point, she could see Bobby's pier. The view was possible because of the downed fence.

Suddenly, the back door flew open. A short man in clean, wrinkled clothes and new white fisherman boots scowled at the investigator.

"What the hell are you doing in my yard?" The grizzled man asked.

"I saw you peeking through the window. I wasn't sure if a thief had broken in, and I'm checking it out."

"I ain't no thief. I own this place," the man replied.

"I'm Niki Dupre. I'm a private investigator."

The sloppily dressed man with a half-full pouch of Red Man chewing tobacco in his pocket eyed her from head to toe. When he finished, he rubbed his whiskered chin. Then, he spat a stream of brown liquid past the investigator. Some of it dribbled down his chin onto his shirt.

"Niki Dupre, huh? You're that fancy kung fu gal, ain't you? You know, I ain't so bad at that judo karate stuff myself. I took me some lessons when I was a tadpole."

Niki didn't want to inform him about the vast difference between judo and karate. Or that her discipline was in Kempo, with finishing touches of *tae kwon do* for its powerful leg techniques.

"Do you have proof that you live here?" She asked.

"I ain't gotta give no proof. Get off my property 'fore I called the cops."

Niki stuck herself cell forward.

"Samson Mayeaux is the third-speed dial button. He's the Chief of Homicide. Tell him I said *hello* when he answers."

The man looked at the phone the same way he would have a cottonmouth. He took a half step backward before recovering.

"What's he got to do with you being in my yard?"

"I'm investigating the murder of your neighbor, Bobby Burns."

"Bobby's dead?" The man's eyes grew wide.

"He was killed right before or after the storm. We're still trying to pin down the exact time."

"Can't say I'm surprised. That was the most selfish fella I ever knowed."

It was Niki's turn to be taken aback. From everything she knew and had heard about Bobby Burns directly conflicted with this man's assessment. Pattie Grace's husband was widely extolled as a kind and generous gentleman.

"Why do you say he was selfish?" She asked.

"Ain't no secret. Bobby caught way more blue cats than he shoulda. He only left mud cats for the rest of us."

Niki had to consider this. She knew blue catfish were prized for their delicate flavor. Their cousins, the oily mud catfish, were disdained by most serious fishermen.

"I don't understand," the PI said though she knew what he meant. "Can you explain?"

"I kept telling the fool he couldn't keep hogging all the blue cats. The way he caught them left the rest of us with the trash fish."

"From what I've been told, the fish population is

limited by the amount of food available, not by harvesting."

"There you go. That's what I'd expect a city girl to think. You don't know nothing 'bout fishing."

Niki didn't bother to tell the man her father and Samson had taken her fishing and hunting every available opportunity. If she wasn't pulling in a bream, bass, catfish, or sac-a-lait, she was aiming at a squirrel, rabbit, turkey, dove or deer.

"I saw the feeders on his pier. The amount of food he fed them added more catfish to the population than he could have possibly caught," she said.

"That ain't true even if he was dumb enough to fill 'em up right before the storm hit. He was always inviting a bunch of folks from his church over for fish fries."

"Did he ever invite you?"

"I didn't go to his church." The man spat another stream of tobacco and slammed the door.

CHAPTER TWELVE

"What did you find out about that character?" Niki asked. She was back at her townhouse with Donna.

"His name is David *Fuzzy* Wild. I couldn't find the origin of the nickname."

"It's not his fuzzy personality," Niki laughed. "He borders on obnoxious."

"More than bordering if you want to believe his neighbors. He's filed lawsuits against every home-owner on Bayou Delaune."

"Let me guess," Niki said. "He believes they're all catching too many catfish."

"Bingo. Specifically, blue catfish. Looks like he has an obsession about them."

"I've seen some professional fishermen I would describe as overly obsessed, but they fish for a living. They have to be overboard, or they wouldn't be good at what they do."

"Well, Mr. Wild is a professional pain in the butt," Donna said. "And he's more than good at being one."

"Has he done anything beyond filing lawsuits?"

"Hold on." Donna scrolled down the pages on the monitor. "He shot a hole in the bottom of one neighbor's bateau. He set another man's boathouse on fire. He..."

"I get the picture," Niki interrupted. "Can you figure out where he was when the storm hit? Also, how he has electricity when nobody else in the subdivision does?"

"The second question is easy. He has a whole-house generator. It automatically kicks on when the electricity fails. Powers the entire home, and he doesn't have to do anything."

"Wow. It's quiet. I didn't hear a thing."

"For your second question." Donna scrolled further down the online data. "He checked into Stumble Inn in Lafayette at one o'clock the afternoon before Brenda hit."

"That's an hour west of Watson. That means he had to leave at noon or before."

"Before," Donna replied. "He stopped in Henderson to eat on the way. Had the catfish platter and bought some chewing tobacco on the way out."

"I should've known he'd have the catfish. What else would Fuzzy Wild eat?"

"I'd guess it took him forty-five minutes to get to Henderson. That means he had to leave Watson around ten-fifteen if it took him an hour to order and eat."

"That pretty well rules him out for Bobby's murder. It's hard to smash a man's head long distance. What did you find about the kids?"

CHAPTER THIRTEEN

"I DIDN'T FIND any evidence Gary left Bernie. Instead, he bought groceries up there around seven that night."

"It's a four-hour trip. I guess we can strike him from our list."

"Mary left town early. She and her family checked into a hotel in Alexandria around three that afternoon," Donna said.

"I never seriously considered her a suspect," Niki replied. "With her medical issues, I don't believe she has the strength to hit her dad that hard."

"That brings us to Dena. She was definitely in town right before Brenda. She bought gas and a Po' boy at Frogs. That's a convenience store five miles from Bobby's home."

"Yeah, I've had their Po' boys. Not bad at all."

"Have you found anything about her relationship with Bobby?"

"From all the emails, texts, and Instagram postings, she loved her father. I found nothing to indicate there was a problem between them."

"What she at Bobby's house the night of the murder?" Niki asked.

"I can put her in the neighborhood," Donna responded. "She made a phone call from her cell phone about an hour before Hurricane Brenda blew across Watson."

"That makes her a suspect. Is there anything in her background that would suggest fits of anger?"

"She struck a boyfriend way back in high school. Evidently, he tried to do something she didn't like. According to the school report, she laid him out."

"Sounds like a girl who can take care of herself. I wonder if she and Bobby had some sort of argument."

"That, I can't tell you. I can only tell you she was around Bobby's house about the time he was murdered."

"I guess that brings us to Donald. Did you find anything interesting about him?"

CHAPTER FOURTEEN

"Donald has some issues. He is extremely reserved but tends to lash out at those opposed to him," Donna told Niki.

"Give me some examples," Niki said.

"In high school, a kid on the football team took a cheap shot at him. When the coaches pulled Donald off the youngster, they had to call an ambulance."

"Wow. What did the coaches do to Donald?"

"Nothing. They said the kid that was hurt deserved what he got. They supported Donald all the way. I guess it was because he was the best player on the team."

"We've seen that kind of cover-up right here at our university. What else do you have?" Niki asked.

"His first year in the Navy didn't go so well. He tended to scuffle with his superiors regularly."

"It sounds like he has a disrespect for authority," Niki said.

"It doesn't only sound like it," Donna responded. "He downright hates it. He can't stand for someone to tell him what to do."

"Would that include Bobby?"

"You betcha. He and Bobby had more than one physical disagreement."

"By that, do you mean they got into fights?" Niki asked.

"Yep. When Donald was young, meaning his teenage years, he and Bobby got into several altercations. Bobby won every one of those."

"And what happened when Donald got older?"

"Bobby didn't win the last altercation. He ended up in the hospital with a broken arm and a separated shoulder."

"Are you sure Donald did that to him?"

"The police report said so. Bobby refused to press charges, but the cops took statements from both Bobby and Donald."

"What was the fight about?"

"Bobby said something about Donald's wife. The report doesn't say exactly the words he used, but they must have been less than complimentary."

"Did Donald sustain any injuries?"

"Only if you consider a bruised fist an injury," Donna laughed. "He had two of them."

"It sounds like I need to talk to Donald," Niki said.

CHAPTER FIFTEEN

Donald Burns lived outside of Watson. His ranch-style house sat on forty-two acres of prime real estate. A stream ran through the middle of the oak-laden bottom. The long driveway led to the large double front doors.

Niki wasn't sure what the young man might be like other than the information she received from Donna's research. That data showed that Donald could be explosive despite his reserved nature. In times of stress, he had struck out at various people, including his superiors in the Navy.

When she knocked on the door, Niki was surprised the remote ranch had electricity. Then she remembered that David Wild had a home generator. She assumed that Donald also had one.

When he opened the door, the investigator had to look up at the tanned man. He stood a good ten inches above the long-legged PI. Bobby's son had no fat. Muscles rippled from his exposed biceps. In his mid-thirties, Donald had the physique of someone fifteen years younger. His physical presence must have daunted those around him.

"I'm Niki Dupre. I'm investigating the death of your father," Niki said as an introduction.

Donald said nothing. His expression revealed no indication about his thoughts. He continued to stand in the doorway.

"May I come in?" Niki asked.

Again, Donald remained quiet. However, he stepped aside and opened the door further. Niki entered the foyer, more nervous than she had been on the way there. She couldn't explain her unease, only that she was not comfortable in Donald's presence.

The tall man walked toward the living room. It resembled a taxidermy shop with stuffed mounts of deer, turkeys, squirrels, an elk, and a moose. There was little doubt Donald enjoyed the outdoors.

Niki sat in a large wooden rocker that was big enough to fit two of the lean investigator. Donald plopped into a recliner. He turned off the television that was on Fox News.

"Did you see your father the day he died?" Niki asked.

"Yes."

"What time did you see him?"

"In the afternoon," Donald again was terse.

"Can you be more specific?"

"Nope."

"I need to find out precisely the timeline for Bobby that afternoon. You can help establish that," Niki said.

Donald said nothing. He continued to stare at the investigator.

"Are you willing to help me?"

"Yep."

"Then you must tell me what time you were there," Niki said.

"In the afternoon," Donald repeated.

"Was it after three o'clock?"

"Yep."

"Was it before six o'clock?"

"Yep."

"So, it was between three and six. Can you narrow it down anymore?"

"Nope."

"Did you try to convince your father to leave before the hurricane hit?" Niki asked.

"Yep."

"What did he say?"

"Not much."

"Why did he want to stay when he knew what was coming?"

"His fish."

"Do you mean the catfish he fed at the dock?"

"Yep."

"Why did he want to protect them? Didn't he know they would be okay in the bayou?"

Donald shrugged his shoulders. He gave no verbal response.

"Did you guys get into an argument?"

"Yep."

"Did it turn physical?"

"Yep."

"Can you tell me exactly what happened?" Niki asked.

"Nope."

"Did Bobby get hurt in the altercation?"

"Yep."

"Did you hit him with a hammer?"

"Nope."

"Where did you hit him?"

Another shrug. Donald's face remained expressionless.

"You have to know where Bobby got hurt. Why can't you tell me?"

"It's none of your business."

CHAPTER SIXTEEN

Dena's home resembled those Niki played with as a child. It was picture-book designed, trim and proper in every respect. The yard had been cleaned up since the storm and looked immaculate. Every blade of grass was the same height. Every remaining bush and flower stood erect in the ornate beds abutting the house.

Dena answered at the first knock. She had a portable generator running, and the electrical cord ran to a multiple outlet. From there, cords ran to the refrigerator, the television, and a large portable air conditioner. An air bed had been placed on the floor in the den. From the size, Niki figured Dena and her husband would fit on it.

The youngest of the children looked younger than she was. Dena could have passed for twenty-five or less. Her bright smile contrasted with her brother's reserved countenance.

"I'm Niki Dupre. I'm..."

"I know who you are," Dena interrupted. "You're looking into my dad's death. Come on in, and I'll make some coffee."

Niki followed the outgoing young lady to a loveseat opposite a large recliner. The chair was much more comfortable than the rocker at Donald's ranch.

"You don't have to make coffee," Niki said. "I know how inconvenient it is when the power is out."

"I don't mind," Dena replied. "We have gas burners, and I can boil some water in a jiffy. We still use the old-style drip pots. We like the coffee a lot better in those."

"I haven't had coffee made in one of those for years," Niki laughed. "But I don't want you to go to the trouble. I only have a few questions."

"Sure. What do you want to know?"

"Were you in the neighborhood when Bobby was killed?"

"No. We stayed here to ride out the storm. We knew it might be bad, but we didn't want to leave our house. Too many people leave and have nothing left when they return."

"Weren't you scared?" Niki asked.

"Our faith removes all fear. We believe our fate is in God's hands. We trust Him in everything we do."

"But doesn't He expect you to make good decisions? Staying with a hurricane coming doesn't sound like a good decision to me," Niki said.

"Was Saul's decision to become Paul and become the greatest missionary of all time a safe decision?"

"I think that was a little different," Niki said, shaking her head. "How many people can you witness to in the eye of the storm?"

"A lot of people knew we were staying. They also knew why we were staying. I believe our faith and our actions were examples for them."

"Okay. I got a little off track. You said you weren't

in the neighborhood when Bobby was murdered. Is that right?"

"I've already said we were hunkered down here. I don't believe I left any doubt," Dena replied.

"Then, who used your phone that night?"

For the first time, Dena's smile faded. She took a glance at Niki, then stared at her shoes. She didn't respond to Niki's question.

"We know your phone was in Bobby's subdivision. If you didn't loan it to someone, that means you were in his subdivision also."

Tears formed in the corner of Dena's eyes. A small one ran down her cheeks and dropped on her blouse. Still, she said nothing.

"Why are you hiding the fact that you were there? What are you covering up?"

The tears increased. Dena's body shook in the recliner. Her lips quivered as though she was trying to form words. None came out.

"You know something that you're not telling," Niki said. "It may help us solve the murder of your father. Why won't you tell me what you saw?"

"I can't." Dena walked out of the back door.

CHAPTER SEVENTEEN

Bruce Daniels displayed a more upbeat tone than the last time he had talked to Niki. That made the private investigator more nervous.

"Hello, Niki," he beamed. "Have you been busy doing my job for me?"

"I've been busy, but I've been doing my job," Niki replied.

"I bet you didn't find out what I did. Would you like to take the bet?"

"I have no idea what you found, Bruce. That sounds like a sucker bet to me."

Bruce laughed. "You can say it's a sucker bet. But it doesn't really matter if you take it or not. You'll have to admit I won after you hear what I discovered."

"It sounds like you can't wait to tell me," Niki responded. "Why don't you go ahead and spit it out?"

"Do you remember the hammer? The murder weapon I'm talking about? Do you remember that it had blood on it?"

"I know about that. The blood the belonged to Bobby Burns."

"And that's the key to my discovery. Guess whose fingerprints we found on the hammer."

"That's old news," Niki said. "We already know that Pattie Grace's prints were on the handle. She has a perfectly good explanation for that."

"I bet she came up with one. However, she's going to have a hard time explaining the new evidence."

"Will you quit beating around the bush and tell me what you found?"

"We found Mrs. Burns's prints in her husband's blood on the tool."

Niki took a sharp intake of air. This was something that Pattie Grace had not explained. The petite woman had told her she had picked up the hammer and threatened her husband with it. However, she didn't say it had Bobby's blood on it at the time.

"What do you plan on doing?" Niki asked.

"We plan on having her arrested in Bernice. Then, we'll transport her back to South Louisiana. That is, unless she wants to drive down here and turn herself in."

"Let me talk to her. Maybe she has an explanation for her prints in Bobby's blood. I'm not sure what it would be, but I want to give her the chance to explain."

CHAPTER EIGHTEEN

"Miss Pattie Grace, you lied to me. Why did you do that?" Niki asked over her cell phone.

"I have never lied to you," the widow replied. "What are you talking about?"

"Your prints are on the hammer. You didn't tell me you held it after Bobby died."

Pattie Grace said nothing for a long time. Niki could hear her pace of breathing elevating. She wondered what was going on in her former Sunday School teacher's mind. It didn't take long to find out.

"I went back to the house."

"No joke. We've already figured that out. Why did you kill Bobby?" Niki asked.

"I didn't. He was already dead when I got there."

"That kite won't fly," Niki said. "You're prints are in Bobby's blood. I can only think of one way how they got there."

"You're wrong," Pattie Grace cried. "I walked in and saw him by the back door."

"Why didn't you call the police? Isn't that what a normal person would do?"

"I told you that I panicked. I saw the hammer by his body. I can't explain to you why I picked it up, but I did."

"That makes no sense to me, Miss Pattie Grace. Why would you pick up a bloody hammer when your husband is laying on the floor dead?"

"I told you that I wasn't thinking clearly. After I picked it up, I knew what it would look like. I knew that I would be arrested for my husband's death."

"What did you do after you picked up the hammer?"

"I took it with me. I wanted to get rid of the evidence. But then, I didn't want them to find it in my car. So, I put it on a shelf in the garage."

"Why did you do that?"

"I figured with the hurricane coming, no one would find it out there. Plus, our house shouldn't have survived the storm. We were directly in the path."

"I hope you realize that the cops won't buy your story," Niki said.

"Niki, you've known me since you were thirteen years old. Have you ever known me to lie to you?"

"Yes. You told me you left Watson at three o'clock in the afternoon. Now, I know you didn't. I would consider that a bald-faced lie."

"I was scared. I didn't want to admit I was there after Bobby died. If he hadn't have stayed for those stupid fish, he would've been on the way to Bernice with me. Now, look where I'm at."

"You're in a heap of trouble," Niki replied. "I'm on your side, and I'm not sure I believe your explanation, especially after you lied to me the first time."

"Niki, you've got to help me. I didn't kill Bobby. I

loved him even though sometimes he cared for those catfish more than me."

"I'm not sure what I can do, Miss Pattie Grace. The evidence is stacked against you."

CHAPTER NINETEEN

Niki's mood turned dour. She moped around her townhome, even with the perky Donna Cross trying to uplift her spirits. The hourglass blonde did everything she could to penetrate the dark clouds surrounding her friend.

"I've got a couple of doughnuts left if that will help," Donna said.

Niki didn't bother to look up. She kept pacing back and forth behind the couch. Doughnuts wouldn't solve the problem. She wasn't sure what would.

"How can we explain Miss Pattie Grace's prints?" She asked.

"I don't think my skills are meant for that," Donna replied. "Unless it's in a database on the Internet, I'm not sure I can help. You're the problem solver in this relationship."

"I never thought she would lie to me. Of all the people in the world, she's probably the one I trusted the most."

"When the pressure gets too big, anyone will lie. It

just takes a certain amount, and that is different for each of us."

"You've never lied to me," Niki said. "And you've been under a whole bunch of pressure, sometimes with your life at stake."

"I lied to myself. Do you remember when I was dating the football player when we first met?"

"Of course, I do. He was a real jerk. I don't know what you saw in him."

"That's what I mean. He was an obnoxious imbecile, but I kept telling myself he was the man of my dreams. I don't think lying gets any bigger than that."

"What can we do?" Niki asked.

"Find the killer if you don't believe that it's Pattie Grace."

"I'm not sure now. A few hours ago, I would have sworn on a stack of Bibles that she was incapable of murder. However, I also thought she was incapable of telling me a story that wasn't true."

"Do you want to tell her that you're no longer on this case?"

"I can't do that. As much as she hurt me by lying, I still consider her among the best people I've ever known. Even if she murdered Bobby, I have to find out the truth. I wouldn't rest without knowing."

CHAPTER TWENTY

Sweat broke out on the man's brow. And under his armpits. And in the small of his back. He felt like a worm in a fish tank. Sitting behind the bush outside of Niki's townhome was the worst situation he could imagine. He thought back to how he got into this predicament.

He owed money. Not a lot, but more than he could afford to pay. The people who he owed had grown impatient with his excuses. He tried to come up with new ones. They told him he would need new knees unless he came up with the dough.

When he was approached about killing Niki Dupre, he wanted no part of it. He had heard about the most famous investigator in Louisiana. He knew about her expertise in Kempo. He knew others had tried to kill her, and all had failed.

That's one reason he felt so incompetent holding an eight-inch hunting knife as his only weapon. The blade was sharp. He had honed it for over an hour the night before. That wasn't the problem. The problem was having the courage to attack an unarmed woman. It went against his nature.

But getting his knees turned backward also went against his nature, more so than attacking a female. He had only two options, and both were bad. He chose the one that would get him free of the other problem. After he killed Niki Dupre, the debt would be settled, and he could go back to life as usual.

Even in the cool morning air, he couldn't stop sweating. He knew it came from fear. He didn't need to see the sweat to know he was scared. His hands quivered. A tic formed in his left bloodshot eye. As much as he tried to stop them, his legs continued to tremble.

He wasn't sure he could rise to the occasion. Literally. He didn't trust his shaking legs to vault from behind the bush. However, he had no choice. He had committed to do this. He couldn't back out now.

When the door to the townhouse opened, he stiffened. He knew the moment was at hand. There was no turning back. His hand gripped the hilt of the knife so hard that his fingers turned white.

He panted so loud he was afraid the strawberry blonde would hear. When she closed the door behind her, he saw Niki reached into her purse to grab her SUV keys. When she took two steps forward, the hired thug leaped from behind his cover. He was only two feet from his target.

He brought the knife down, intending to slam it between her shoulder blades. Only, her shoulder blades were no longer there. Somehow, Niki Dupre had sensed his presence. Or the danger. He didn't know which. He only knew she had realized someone attempted to do her harm and had reacted.

His momentum took him forward. A kick below his kneecap made him stumble. His attempt to thrust the knife into her body made the weapon cross his own. He tried to pull it back. He was only partly successful. The blade buried in his chest, penetrating part of a lung and his lower heart. He no longer had to worry about paying his debts.

CHAPTER TWENTY-ONE

Samson lumbered back and forth outside the tape marking the crime scene and the dead body. He kept shaking his head. His young friend, Niki Dupre, seemed to attract this kind of attention. Not the right kind.

"Do you know who he is?" Niki asked.

"His name is Ricky Johnson. He is currently unemployed and has been known to frequent some of the less than elite establishments that serve alcohol."

"Why did he try to kill me?" The private investigator asked.

"I'd guess someone paid him," the Chief of Homicide replied.

Niki sighed. She had three prime suspects in the murder of Bobby Burns. His wife, Pattie Grace. His son, Donald. His daughter, Dena. The investigator had a hard time believing any would hire an assassin to kill her. Well, maybe Donald. He had been less than friendly when Niki visited. Donna had discovered that he had been in the vicinity right before Bobby was murdered.

"Did he have any notes or maybe a phone number on him?"

Samson shook his massive head. "Nothing that would lead us back to the person who hired him. He doesn't even have a cell phone. I thought everybody had one of those after they went to kindergarten these days."

"Sometimes, I wish I could lose mine," Niki said. "But then, I'd be out of business. That's how my clients contact me."

"We can try to trace the GPS in his car to see where he was the last couple of days. I'm not sure my guys can do that quickly."

"That's okay. I know someone who has that expertise and is more than willing to use it."

"You've got to quit getting Donna to hack into databases. One day, somebody will find out what she's doing, and it could have repercussions on you."

"Donna and I have had that conversation on numerous occasions. I don't believe she would quit even if she didn't work with me. She loves the challenge of finding information people are trying to hide."

"I hope she finds what she's looking for," Samson said. "You know I can't use whatever she finds officially. The defense lawyer would throw me out on my ear."

"If I find out who hired this man to kill me, you won't have to bother about throwing him in jail. There won't be enough left of him to fit into one of those ugly uniforms."

CHAPTER TWENTY-TWO

"Were you able to find anything about Ricky Johnson?" Niki asked Donna.

"Not a whole lot. He maxed out all of his credit cards at the local bars. He doesn't own a home, and I can't find where he's renting a place," the hourglass blonde responded.

"He had to run into one of our suspects somewhere," Niki said. "We have to find out where."

"Hold on and let me scroll down a few pages. Maybe I can find something that will tie him to one of them."

Niki fixed another pot of coffee. The dark brew, despite the caffeine, tended to settle her nerves. For some reason, when someone attempted to kill her, she was less than serene.

She brought a cup to Donna, who was busily staring at her laptop, going through more pages than Niki could keep up with. The private investigator admired her friend's ability to go through millions of bytes of data to get to the desired end.

"I think I have something," Donna looked up at Niki.

"What is it?" Hope in the investigator's voice.

"He has been staying at the homeless shelter on Airline Highway. From what I can tell, he's been there for several weeks."

"I guess I'll have to take a visit down there and find out who his friends are."

"I think I can help you there. That's why it took so long for me to give you an answer. A couple of our suspects help feed the folks there," Donna said.

"I would bet it's not Donald. That only leaves Pattie Grace and Dena. Am I right?"

"Bingo. Both of them have been working at the shelter for several years. They had to run into Ricky Johnson there. I guess you're down to two suspects now."

"And one of them lied to me. The other left me hanging when I asked her a question. I'm not sure which is at the top of my list now."

CHAPTER TWENTY-THREE

Pattie Grace didn't look like the lady who taught Niki in Sunday school more than a decade ago. She was at the Sheriff's office, turning herself in for the murder of her husband. Her shoulders sagged. Bags formed beneath her eyes. Her red hair stood in disarray. Niki watched her former teacher enter the reception room at the parish prison. She almost felt sorry for the lady. However, Pattie Grace had lied to her. If she lied to her about her presence at the time of the murder, could she have also lied to her about committing it?

The private investigator stood to meet the lady she once admired so much. No matter what Pattie Grace had done in this instance, she had helped Niki become the person she was. That meant a lot to the strawberry blonde.

"I didn't expect you to be here," Pattie Grace said.

"You asked me to help you find the murderer. I told you I would. I try to keep my word," Niki replied.

"But I lied to you. Why do you want to help me now?"

"You know that I admire you and respect you. We

all can falter under pressure. I hope that you will be straightforward from now on."

A tear rolled down Pattie Grace's cheek. She stepped forward and hugged the private investigator. She laid her head on Niki's shoulder.

"I'll try to help you," Niki said. "Tell me the truth, and don't leave anything out."

They sat in adjacent chairs in the reception area. The deputies left them to themselves, allowing Pattie Grace to speak without being overheard. The petite lady told Niki essentially the same story she had before. A few details varied, but the gist of the story remained intact.

"Why didn't you tell me you worked at the homeless shelter?" Niki asked when Pattie Grace finished.

The former teacher looked up in surprise.

"Why is that important? I've been doing that for years."

"Did you meet a gentleman by the name of Ricky Johnson while you worked there?" Niki asked.

"I met a bunch of fellows there. Some of them went by the name Ricky. I never asked for last names," Pattie Grace responded.

"This one was about five feet eight inches and weighed around a hundred and fifty pounds. He had a history of drinking too much."

Pattie Grace shook her head. "That sounds like almost every man I met at the shelter. Why are you asking about this one?"

"He tried to kill me," Niki replied.

Pattie Grace gasped. She looked at Niki with an open mouth.

"Are you sure you didn't know him?" Niki asked.

"I might have met him. But I met several hundred

men during the time I've helped at the shelter. I can't tell you whether I knew him or not. I certainly wasn't close to him."

"Did you hire him to kill me?" Niki asked.

Pattie Grace could only shake her head before the deputy came to arrest her.

CHAPTER TWENTY-FOUR

DENA'S HOUSE looked the same as it had the first time Niki visited. The private investigator could only envy the neatness of it compared to her townhome. When Niki was involved in a case, housework was less of a priority. Donna was too involved searching various databases to lend a hand with cleaning.

"Dena, the last time I was here, you walked out on me," Niki said after being seated.

Dena looked at the floor. Niki was afraid the attractive young lady would walk out again.

"I couldn't tell you the answer to your question," Dena replied.

"Why not?"

"It's not for me to cast aspersions on another family member," Dena said while squirming in her chair.

Niki considered the answer. She came up with two possible scenarios.

"Did you see your mother or your brother leaving Bobby's house when you got there?"

Dena sat still, not moving a muscle. She lifted her gaze from the floor to meet Niki's eyes.

"I won't tell you that. They are both my family. I don't want to blame either of them for Dad's death."

"But it means one of them may be responsible. Wouldn't your dad want you to tell me what you saw?"

"I don't know," Dena responded. "I only know that I've lost my dad. I don't want to lose my mother or my brother."

"Even if they killed your father?"

"If one of them did, they did it on an impulse. My mother and Donald wouldn't hurt Dad under normal circumstances."

"On another subject, how long have you worked at the homeless shelter on Airline Highway?"

Dena looked at Niki with surprise before answering. "My mom talked me into that. Once I got there, I loved it. A lot of people are not as fortunate as I am. I enjoy helping them."

"Did you meet a fellow by the name of Ricky Johnson while working there?"

"Yes. He was going through a difficult time," Dena said.

"Tell me more."

"He had a drinking problem and a gambling issue. He owed money to some folks who were pressing for payments. He asked me if I would loan him some money."

"Did you?" Niki asked.

"No. I talked it over with Mom, and she said not to. She said if I once lent money to him, he would keep asking."

"Pattie Grace knew about Ricky Johnson's problems?"

"I'm not sure if I ever mentioned his name. I only told my mom that it was a guy from the shelter."

"What did you say?" Niki asked.

"She only told me to let it go. She never got involved in the personal lives of the people at the shelter."

"Did you mention it to anyone else?"

Dena hesitated. For a moment, Niki thought she might shut down. However, after a few seconds, she answered the question.

"I told Donald."

"What did he say?"

"He said he would talk to Ricky and tell him to leave me alone. I don't know if he ever did or not."

CHAPTER TWENTY-FIVE

Donald exhibited even less openness with Niki than the first time they talked. If anything, he was more reserved. He continued to eat the crawfish while Niki talked. He took his time to dip them in a hot sauce before putting them in his mouth. After fifteen minutes of dragging answers out of the strong man, Niki grew exasperated.

"What are you hiding, Donald?" She asked. "You aren't telling me anything. Why are you being so secretive?"

The answer came in the form of a shrug. Niki decided to bluff.

"Dena told me she saw you coming out of Bobby's house. It was right before the storm hit. Did you kill him?"

Donald took another crawfish. He dipped it in the hot sauce and started to put it in his mouth. Niki almost screamed.

"Why don't you quit eating and answer my questions?"

Donald's hand paused, and a dab of hot sauce

dropped onto his shirt. Something clicked in Niki's mind, but she couldn't bring the idea to fruition.

"I was there to talk Dad into leaving with Mom," Donald said, using more words than he had in the entire conversation.

"Did you get into a fight with him?"

"You already know that. Why ask again?"

"Because Dena saw you right before the storm hit. Your dad died about that time."

"How do you know that?" Donald asked.

"Because of his stomach contents. He and your mom had Chinese for lunch. He had Kung Pao Shrimp that had peanuts in it. He died about six hours after having that meal."

"I swear I left after we got into a fight. Dad was okay. I didn't hurt him."

Donald tried to wipe the dab of hot sauce from his shirt. He was only successful in smearing it. Instantly, the idea that had been below Niki's consciousness came to the forefront. She knew who murdered Bobby Burns and how to prove it.

Niki rang the doorbell. She heard the chimes inside the home. After the first time, she received no response. She turned to Bruce Daniels.

"I know he's here. He'll have to open the door, or we'll go inside anyway."

"We can't do that. I have to go by the protocol from the Sheriff's office. I can't bust into houses without a warrant," Bruce replied.

Niki turned and banged on the door as hard as she could. This time, she got a response. The man opened the door and glared at both Niki and Bruce.

"What are you guys doing here disturbing me like this?" Fuzzy Wild asked.

Niki didn't bother to answer the question. She pushed inside. Bruce hesitated for a moment, then followed her.

"You can't come into my house!" Wild yelled.

"Yes, we can," Niki replied. "You killed Bobby Burns, and Bruce is here to arrest you."

Niki didn't bother to look at the detective. She had not told him what she was about to do, only that he needed to come along with her. He had agreed after she threatened to tell Samson if he didn't.

"I ain't killed nobody," Fuzzy replied. "Now, get out of my house."

"When we go, you'll be going with us. In hand-cuffs," Niki said.

Fuzzy took a step back. He looked first at Niki and then at Bruce. Then he addressed the private investigator.

"You can't say that. That's slander. I can sue you in court."

"Like you've sued your neighbors for catching too many catfish? How many have you sued?"

"That ain't none of your business. It don't matter none."

"This time, you went too far. You got into an argument with Bruce over the number of fish he caught. When he turned his back on you, you picked up the hammer on the counter and hit him with it," Niki remained calm.

"That ain't true. You ain't got no proof."

"You told me he fed his fish right before the storm. I checked the feeders, and you were right. The one without power was filled to the brim. He had to pour the feed in it minutes before the storm hit. The only way for you to know that is if you were in his house watching him. You wouldn't have been able to see him from your property because of the fence."

"The fence was torn down in the storm. You ain't got nothing."

"But it was up until after Bobby fed the fish."

"So what? That still ain't no proof."

"I've got all the proof I need. You put on your new

boots and threw the old ones away. There must have been blood on the old ones."

"My old boots wore out. I had to get some new ones. Wearing new boots don't prove I killed Bobby," Fuzzy said.

"I agree," Niki responded. "You probably also washed your clothes because they had blood on them."

"Ain't no law against washing clothes. I try to keep clean."

"But you forgot something. Something that will prove you killed Bobby."

Fuzzy's eyes went wide. He looked around the room as if trying to find the incriminating evidence. When he couldn't, he turned back to Niki.

"What the hell are you talking about?"

"That pack of chewing tobacco in your pocket. You bought it in Henderson the day of the storm. You checked into the hotel and then decided to return to your house."

"So what? That don't prove nothing," Fuzzy exclaimed.

"Pull out the pack of tobacco and give it to Bruce," Niki said.

"Why? I ain't gotta do that."

"If you don't, I'll take it from you," Niki said.

Fuzzy put up his hands in a classic kung fu stance. Niki almost giggled.

"You don't want to do that, Mr. Wild. You don't stand a chance."

"I told you I took lessons as a kid. I didn't get no belt, but I was better than anybody in there."

"Trust me," Niki said with a grin. "There's nothing I would like better than to beat you to a pulp. You hired Ricky Johnson to kill me. You probably met him in a bar and bought him a drink."

"So what? I meet a lot of people in bars. I don't remember their names most of the time."

"But you remember Ricky Johnson. You agreed to pay off his debts if he would kill me."

Fuzzy lunged at Niki. It was a feeble attempt. In less than five seconds, the fight was over. Wild lay on the dirty floor on his back. Niki reached in his pocket and pulled out the back of tobacco. She handed it to Bruce.

"What am I supposed to do with this?" Bruce asked.

"You'll find Bobby's blood on it. When Mr. Wild hit Bobby, he raised the hammer again. Splatter got on his shirt and boots. It also got on the pack of tobacco."

Bruce examined the aluminum package. He spotted the specks of blood that had fallen on it during the attack on Bobby. He reached over and cuffed David *Fuzzy* Wild's hands.

Dear reader,

We hope you enjoyed reading *Murder Hammers!*. Please take a moment to leave a review, even if it's a short one. Your opinion is important to us.

Discover more books by Jim Riley at https://www.nextchapter.pub/authors/jim-riley

Want to know when one of our books is free or discounted? Join the newsletter at http://eepurl.com/bqqB3H

Best regards,

Jim Riley and the Next Chapter Team

NOTES

Murder Hammers! is the sixteenth of over twenty short mysteries in the Niki Dupre series. It features the dynamic martial arts expert facing even more significant challenges.

I have taken a tremendous literary license with the geography and data of Baton Rouge and the surrounding areas. It is a beautiful city and a great way to experience Cajun culture. I live there and find it one of the most desirable places on earth if you enjoy the outdoors, excellent cuisine, and remarkable people.

There are so many people to thank:

My family, Linda, Josh, Dalton & Jade

David and Sara Sue

C D and Debbie Smith

My brother and sister-in-law, Bill & Pam

My sister, Debbie

My sister-in-law and her husband, Brenda & Jerry

The Sunday School class at Zoar Baptist

My cousin, Pattie Grace, for the use of her name. She is truly a fine lady.

Jeff Trout and Chris Hall, two real men who stood beside me during my darkest hours. Jeff tried to teach me about Kempo, the ancient Chinese martial art. He soon found out I'm a slow learner.

Any mistakes, typos, and errors are my fault and mine alone. If you would like to get in touch with me, go to my website at http://jimriley.net.

I thank you for reading **Murder Hammers!** and hope you enjoy the rest of my books.

Murder Hammers!
ISBN: 978-4-82411-851-6
Mass Market

Published by
Next Chapter
1-60-20 Minami-Otsuka
170-0005 Toshima-Ku, Tokyo
+818035793528

28th November 2021